Prisoners of the Scrambling Dragon

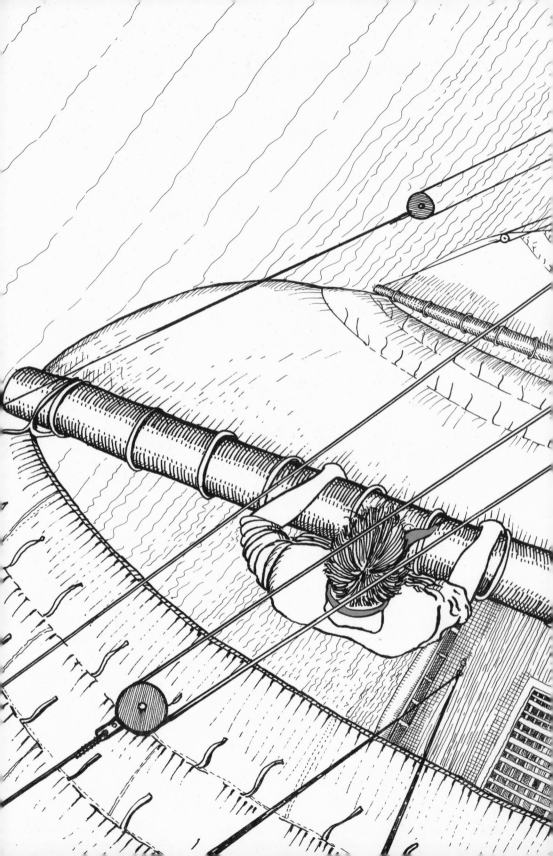

Prisoners
of the
Scrambling
Dragon

by F. N. MONJO

illustrated by Arthur Geisert

Holt, Rinehart and Winston / New York

Acknowledgments

Special thanks are due to Francis Ross Carpenter, formerly assistant director of the Museum of the American China Trade in Milton, Massachusetts, for helping me with the Chinese characters used in the text, and for enlightening me in so many of the details of the intricacies of the China trade, the character of Houqua, and many other matters. I should also like to thank Sylvia C. Hilton and the staff of the New York Society Library (where most of the research for this book was done) for their continuing help on so many occasions.

F.N.M.

Text copyright © 1980 by Nicolas Adam Monjo
Illustrations copyright © 1980 by Arthur Geisert
Published simultaneously in Canada by Holt, Rinehart
and Winston of Canada, Limited.
Printed in the United States of America

10 9 8 7 6 5 4 3 2 1

Library of Congress Cataloging in Publication Data
Monjo, F. N.   Prisoners of the scrambling dragon.
SUMMARY: A 13-year-old cabin boy describes
his first voyage aboard a Yankee trading vessel, bound
for China during the 1820's, carrying furs, silver,
ginseng, sandalwood, and opium.
[1. China—Commerce—Fiction.   2. United States—
Commerce—Fiction.   3. Voyages and travels—Fiction]
I. Geisert, Arthur.   II. Title.   PZ7.M75Pt
[Fic]   79-4449   ISBN 0-03-016656-X

Also by F. N. Monjo

Indian Summer
The Drinking Gourd
The One Bad Thing About Father
Pirates in Panama
The Vicksburg Veteran
The Jezebel Wolf
Slater's Mill
The Secret of the Sachem's Tree
Rudi and the Distelfink
Me and Willie and Pa
Poor Richard in France
Grand Papa and Ellen Aroon
The Sea Beggar's Son
King George's Head Was Made of Lead
Willie Jasper's Golden Eagle
Letters to Horseface
Gettysburg: Tad Lincoln's Story
Zenas and the Shaving Mill
The Porcelain Pagoda
A Namesake for Nathan
The House on Stink Alley

Contents

1 · At Lintin Island　11
2 · On Board the Scrambling Dragon　49
3 · In Canton, at the American Hong　67
About this Story　93

Prisoners of the Scrambling Dragon

·1·
At Lintin Island

Hawk began moaning beside me. I was never so glad to hear such a sound in my life. I thought they might have killed him when they jumped us. It must have been six of the stinking devils. Six or more. It would take at least half a dozen normal-sized men to dare try to mess with Hawk, big as he is. And these had been scrawny little men, from what I had seen.

"Hawk," I whispered. "You all right, Hawk?"

He just murmured and groaned. I wondered how long I'd been unconscious. How long the two of us had been lying here. My hands were tied tight behind me. It was too dark to see anything, here in the hold. I kept hearing the steady lurch and splash of ten or twelve oars. And I could feel the regular dip and rise of the vessel cutting through the waves.

I figured it must still be nighttime. Not that I could have seen anything, even in broad daylight. We were too far down in the hold for that, with no portholes anywhere. Not even a crack of light showing.

"They must have covered us with something," I muttered. It felt like burlap sacking. I couldn't do anything about pulling it off, because my arms were tied too tight. I kept straining against the ropes around my wrists, but that only made my hands hurt worse than before. So after a while I quit struggling.

"Well, Sam," says I to myself, "you really landed yourself in a Number One Piecee predicament *this* time." That's what the old China hands say—"Number One Piecee"—when they mean "first-rate."

Hawk groaned again. He was heaving around in his sleep. His shoulder struck me.

"You awake, Hawk? Hawk, you alright?"

He never answered. I was plenty scared. Here I am, halfway around the world from my Yankee home. Thousands and thousands of miles from Newburyport, Massachusetts. Trussed up like a hog, waiting to be butchered. Lying in the stinking hold of some little Chinese ship. Me and Hawk. The two of us prisoners of a pack of Chinese pirates!

There is no way in the world that this can

be happening to me, I keep telling myself.
Maybe it's just a nightmare. Maybe I don't
have a lump as big as an egg aching behind
my left ear. Maybe I'm just having a wild bad
dream, and I'll wake up safe, back in my bunk
in the forecastle of the *Orient Venture*.

There'd be the smell of bacon or salt pork
frying, drifting in from the galley. And Hawk
Hollings would be sitting there beside me,
singing something cheerful in his deep bass
voice. Playing on that accordion I gave him.
His huge black face just smiling all over . . .

But there isn't any smell of bacon and there
isn't any accordion playing. Only the rustling
of something that may be a rat scrabbling
around in the hold. And Hawk lying trussed
up beside me, still out of his head, lurching
and muttering.

"Watch out for them, Sam!" he's murmur-
ing. His voice is slurred and he's talking wild.
"Yonder they come! They're going to try to
board us!"

Hawk begins thrashing around something
fierce. Cursing in his delirious sleep. Cursing
the pirates who'd come swinging aboard the
Orient Venture. Throwing their stink bombs.
Hurling their grappling hooks up onto the
deck and into the rigging. Setting off firecrackers, in their crazy way. Clenching cut-

lasses in their teeth as they come swirling up at us, screeching, out of the fog.

*   *   *

I'm still too confused and my head keeps aching too hard to remember just how every-thing happened. Or how long ago.

Uncle Hiram had said, all along, that a voyage to China was bound to be fraught with peril. He'd promised us dangers of every kind. Shipwrecks. Monsoons. Even cannibals, maybe, on some of the Pacific islands. Dan-gerous Indians on the Oregon coast. And pirates in the China seas, when we sailed up the bay approaching Canton.

My ma has been a widow for some years now, with a pile of children to raise. And I'm her younger son. Her brother, Captain Hiram Dwight, is skipper of the frigate *Orient Ven-ture*, sailing in the China trade. So Ma couldn't see why Uncle Hiram shouldn't do something to help his nephew, Sam Dwight, get ahead in the world.

"You take advantage of what Uncle Hiram can offer you, Sam Dwight," says Ma, "and you may end up just as rich as him, someday."

Pa hadn't left us much besides the farm when he died. And my older brother, Talcott,

was taking care of *that* just fine, for Ma and the girls.

So there was no reason for me *not* to try my fortune in the China trade, with Uncle Hiram. I'm only just turned thirteen, so I couldn't rate as an honest-to-goodness able seaman. But Uncle Hiram said there was plenty of skippers today, making a fortune sailing to Canton, who started out as cabin boys when they was no older than me.

"And he'll be comin' in through the cabin window, at that, Penelope," says Uncle Hiram to Ma.

By which he meant that I had the advantage of having a close relative in the ship's cabin. When a sailor doesn't have any family connections in the business to help him get ahead, and he has to sign on just as an ordinary seaman, why then folks say he's "coming in by the hawsehole." That means he's going to have to work himself up the hard way. I guess they say that because the hawser, for the anchor, is right up there in the bow, alongside the forecastle, where the ordinary seamen eat and sleep on shipboard.

Anyway, I was crazy eager to go to sea. In through the cabin window. Or up through the hawsehole. Any which way I could do it. It didn't matter to me. I'd been dreaming about sailing to China for years. Without telling Ma and Pa, of course. I think my brother Talcott maybe guessed how I felt, but he never let on to them.

Then, when Pa died, I still didn't say anything about China. Ma's kind of funny that way. If she gets a notion you *want* something real bad, chances are she won't let you have it, if she can help it. It's just the way she is.

When she started urging me to sail to China with Uncle Hiram, while he was getting ready for his third voyage, I just acted like I was sort of indifferent to the whole thing. I said to myself: I'll just let Ma think that she has to persuade *me*. Even though I was aching to sign on and sail.

She kept after me for a whole month, asking me how come any red-blooded boy wouldn't jump at the chance of sailing to Canton? She went on, describing the lines of the *Orient Venture* as if she'd designed them herself, from stem to stern. Reminding me of the eight cannon the ship was carrying, besides two swivel guns, fore and aft. Calculating the huge profits that many a vessel no bigger than the *Orient Venture* has earned, if she can manage to get herself back home, safe, to New England, stuffed with pearls and spices and crates of chinaware, and hundreds of

brassbound chests of sweet-smelling China tea.

I let Ma run on and on. And when she was just about wore out from talking, I said I'd think it over.

It worked real good. Uncle Hiram signed me up, all formal and proper, as if I was a grown man. The papers he drew up said I'd be earning 1/900 of the profits when the *Orient Venture* come home and was warped up safe alongside the Long Wharf in Newburyport harbor. Of course, Uncle Hiram was going to come in for a healthy ⅓ of the profits. But Ma said even *my* tiny little share might earn me $200 or $300—depending on how successful we was.

Lying here, trussed up in this pirate skiff, I keep wondering why it was all of us ever begun calling him Hawk. Hawk isn't his real name. His name is Rufus Hollings. But all of us on the *Orient Venture* always called him Hawk.

He's the biggest man I've ever seen. Ebony black. Thick-bearded. Arms and shoulders all muscled and corded and knotted. Just huge.

We got to be good friends right away. Partly because he was the biggest and I was the shortest, skinniest sailor on board, I suppose. But only partly because of the difference in size. He knew I was only thirteen and he didn't want any of the rest of the men making my life miserable.

"Don't any of you mess with Sam," Hawk would blare, "or you'll all be messing with me."

They were real scared of him—even the men who hated him just for being black—and there was more than a few of them. Mr. Redmond, the first mate, was ever so respectful once he'd took a good look at Hawk's huge fists and shoulders. He didn't let on to be scared, but I watched him close, and I knew.

It was easy to be mindful of Hawk's power. I've seen him slam two men together when they started fighting. And it would be half an hour or more before either one of them come back to his senses.

How Hawk hated any one of them to think he wasn't clean! He'd scrub himself with seawater two and three times a day. Soap and scrub his body all over, and rake himself dry with a towel.

"White man'll tell you niggers stink," Hawk would growl, slashing at his giant body with that soapy sponge. Looked like he wanted to scrub the skin right off himself!

I helped him stay as clean as he wanted to be. I'd go up to the galley, every evening, and get the ship's cook to do me a special favor and heat me up a tub of hot water. Then Hawk and me would sit there, out on deck, under the stars, washing our dirty clothes together. Just the two of us. Washing and talking and talking, while the tub sent up a steamy column of vapor into the cool night sky.

Hawk told me he'd run away from slavery in the South, while Mr. Madison was still President. Six, seven years ago. Stowed away on a coastwise vessel, up from Charleston, sailing into Philadelphia. Wound up in Massachusetts. Claimed he was free. And began shipping out as a sailor.

He said he sailed twice around Africa's Cape of Good Hope, to Calcutta and to Can-

ton. Two or three times to Greece and Turkey, after cargoes of opium. And this voyage on the *Orient Venture* was going to be his third time around Cape Horn, sailing the Pacific, in the China trade.

Strange the way you get to like a man. You couldn't help but notice all that killing muscle, hard-packed, bunched over his huge bones. But anyone who looked carefully at Hawk's eyes was bound to see the pain. That and all the tenderness inside him.

He told me that being big, like he was, sort of kept everybody off, at a distance.

"They figure I want to hurt them," he'd say, with a laugh. But there wasn't any mirth in his laughter. I think I was the only close friend he had.

That's why I gave him my accordion. It was broke, anyway. But Hawk fixed it real good. Then he'd sit with me on deck, at night, after we'd washed our clothes, playing jigs and reels and hymns and hornpipes. And he'd make up songs of his own:

Tell me, little maiden,
Why won't you live with me?
I'm just a lone seafarer
On the ocean sea . . .

Didn't matter whether his songs were about little maidens, or going to Heaven someday, or missing his old home down South, they was almost always sad.

Six months ago, when we'd just rounded the Horn and was beating our way up the coast of Chile, the *Orient Venture* was caught in a terrible, lashing sleet storm. Ice-green waves as high as Pa's barn come slicing over the deck, roaring their fury. One of them caught me and nearly carried me away. But Hawk just wrapped his giant legs around the rail, reached out his huge paws, and plucked me back on shipboard. Just as easy as you'd pick up a pebble off the beach. Or a flower in the meadow. If it hadn't been for Hawk, I'd have been lost for sure. Drowned in that storm off the coast of Chile.

After that, I took orders from Hawk quicker'n I'd take them from Captain Hiram, even. The men in the forecastle laughed about it some. Tried to make me feel foolish and ashamed.

Hawk would holler for me, up on deck.

"Sam! Oh, Sam!"

And one of the men—maybe even Mr. Redmond, the first mate—would give me an evil little grin, and say, "What's the matter, boy?

Can't you hear your pa calling? Better hurry up there and see what he wants."

But they'd never say that where Hawk could hear. Only to me. For a time I used to blush red when they done me so. Then I quit letting it bother me.

* * *

It was a strange, wandering voyage, the voyage of the *Orient Venture*. As Captain Hiram explained it to me—and Hawk explained it further—it wasn't easy to get a trading cargo together that would suit the Chinese. The Chinese feel that they live right smack at the center of the world, with just about everything anybody could want or need spread out thick, all around them, there in the Middle Flowery Kingdom, as they call their land.

The British sent a special ambassador to the Emperor of China not so many years ago. King George III of England was *real* anxious to increase the trade with China. His ambassador carried a letter from the King, practically begging the Chinese to let British ships start trading at all the ports in China.

But the Emperor of China wouldn't *hear* of it. First place, he didn't want "foreign devils" traipsing all over his beautiful kingdom.

That's what they call us Yankees and Europeans: foreign devils! *Fan kwae.* And he wouldn't allow but one of his cities—Canton—to stay open for the trade.

The Emperor went on to say, "We possess all things, and I have no use for your country's manufactures."

It was a bold and haughty reply. Must have made King George puff up with fury.

Still, according to Captain Hiram, there are a few odds and ends that the Chinese *will* accept.

They'll take silver. Pure silver. So Captain Hiram set out prepared, with a few chests of silver dollars stowed away in the hold of the *Orient Venture.* He brought along some bales of ginseng root, too. That's an odd, forked root that grows up north, in the Canadian forests. But the Chinese believe the root has magic powers. So they'll pay plenty for it.

And they love rich, glossy fur—especially sealskins and sea otter. That was why we spent so many weary months sailing up and down the coast, from Oregon to Alaska. Trading furs with the Indians there. Furs bound for the Chinese merchants in Canton.

Seven or eight months later, when we got to Hawaii, Captain Hiram and his supercargo, Dave Woolsey, tried to buy a ton of sandal-

wood. That's a sweet-smelling, oily wood that the Chinese love to burn on the altars of their temples. It grows on the slopes of the volcanoes in the Hawaiian islands. High up, in the cooler air. But the Hawaiian princes have been cutting down the groves of trees so fast that sandalwood is now in mighty short supply. So scarce we had the devil's own time getting hold of just a bit over three hundred pounds of the stuff.

So it's silver and fur and sandalwood and ginseng root that the foreign devils can sell in Canton.

That, and one other wicked substance. Opium.

I don't think Ma knew anything at all about this opium when she was so anxious for me to sign on board the *Orient Venture*. But if it hadn't been for poppy juice and opium, I'm sure Hawk Hollings and me wouldn't be in the fix we're in right now. Captured by Chinese pirates!

* * *

I sure wish Hawk would come to. So I'd know he's all right. He'd know just what to do! He'd start ordering me around, like he always does. Pretty soon we'd both be right as rain. I know we would. But he just keeps muttering, out of his head. I'm lying here with him, under this burlap. Trussed up like a pig or a chicken. Wondering where they're taking us. What they'll do to us next.

Uncle Hiram never told me a thing about how he was shipping opium until the afternoon Hawk Hollings and me found out what was in those chests. By mistake.

We'd been sent down into the after hold of the *Orient Venture*—a couple of months ago—to shift some cargo. There'd been a heavy sea the night before, and some barrels of sealskins had broke loose and rolled about. One of them big barrels had toppled over onto a wooden chest and split its cover open.

"Look at this chest, Hawk," says I. "Looks like it's full of muskmelons. See these big

brown balls of sticky stuff? Must be thirty, forty of 'em."

"I see 'em, Sammy," says Hawk. "But they ain't muskmelons, I can tell you that." His voice rumbled even deeper than usual. The way he does when he's disapproving, or angry.

"Well, what are they, Hawk?"

"Looks like your Uncle Hiram is a smuggling captain, like all the rest," says Hawk, sort of scornful. "That's a chest of Turkish opium, Sammy. And pretty fair quality, too."

Then Hawk told me how the British grow their own huge fields of poppies, for opium, in

India. Slitting the unripened seed capsules of the plants, and scraping off the juice that oozes out. After it dries, they roll the sticky juice into melon-shaped balls. Then smuggle them into China.

"Yankee captains, like your Uncle Hiram," says Hawk, "aren't permitted by the British to trade for opium in India. Because the British want to keep everything they grow there for their *own* selves. So Captain Hiram and the rest of the American skippers have to go to Turkey to buy their opium. But wherever it comes from, most of it winds up in China. Mostly in Canton. I've seen these chests before, so I know what I'm talking about."

Well, you don't argue with Hawk Hollings unless you're prepared for big trouble. Anyway, I've found that he's right much more often than he's wrong.

I couldn't stop thinking about that ugly chest of muskmelons. That same evening, after I'd finished serving Uncle Hiram his supper in his cabin, and he was drinking his coffee and smoking his pipe, I told him what we'd seen, Hawk and I, inside that smashed chest, down in the hold.

"The man's dead right," said Uncle Hiram, real red and angry. "It's Turkish opium, all right. And there's twenty-two more chests, just like it, stowed away down there in that hold. Without them chests of opium, there'd be no profit whatsoever in the China trade, Sam Dwight. Did you have some objection you was thinking of offering?"

Uncle Hiram glared at me real fierce with his cold blue eyes. I'm ashamed to say I didn't *dare* offer him an objection of any kind. But I kept thinking of those chests for a long, long time. Those ugly brown muskmelons. While I was lying in my hammock, later that night, in the forecastle. Swaying back and forth in the darkness. Waiting to fall asleep.

Next day, Captain Hiram told me that he had a struggle with his conscience before he permitted himself to carry opium with him to China.

"It's a devilish bad cargo, Sam Dwight," said he. "The poor heathens smoke the nasty brown stuff, in little opium pipes. Just a single sticky little brown bubble at a time. It's a drug that can bring a poor fellow the sweetest of dreams—for ten or twelve hours at a stretch. But it does untold harm, as well! For soon it takes hold of the man who smokes it. And next thing you know he'll be spending all the money he has for pipe after pipe of opium!"

That's just like my Uncle Hiram. Talking against opium, like it was the most hideous thing in the world. As if he was real worried about it ruining the health and happiness of thousands and thousands of Chinese. Railing about how wicked it is to raise poppies, and all that. And, at the same time, carrying better than twenty chests of opium, destined for Canton, down in the hold of the *Orient Venture*.

Well, no point in being too hard on Captain Hiram. Every skipper in the China trade— all but a handful, anyway—is getting rich smuggling opium to China. Don't make it right, though, that there's so many of them doing it, neither.

A week or two after Hawk and me discovered the chests of opium, we hit the China coast. The *Orient Venture* left the Ladrone Islands to port, and made straight for Macao.

Hawk told me that Macao is a city that was founded hundreds and hundreds of years ago by the Portuguese, when they first came to China to trade. Now there's Dutch and British and Swedes and Yankees living there, too—at least part of the year, when the trade season closes, upriver, in Canton.

Captain Hiram picked up a Chinese pilot in Macao. Then we headed directly north, into

the great blue bay, making for the mouth of the river Pearl.

That night, after we finished washing our clothes, Hawk told me to fetch him a pencil and paper.

"I'm going to draw you a map of the bay, Sam," says he. "So's I can show you the Tiger's Mouth. And Whampoa Reach. And Lintin Island."

"What about Canton?" says I.

"That's way upriver," says Hawk. "Way beyond where this ship can sail. But I'll put in Canton, too."

Hawk bent over his paper, sketching in all the things he wanted to show me. He pointed to an island halfway up the bay. Over it rose the peak of a high, high hill.

"That's Lintin Island," he growled. He tapped the map with his huge thumb. His thumbnail is as big as a quarter!

"Will we be stopping there?"

"Sure will. That's where your Uncle Hiram gets rid of his chests of opium."

"I thought they went upriver to Canton," says I.

"They do," says Hawk, "but not with the rest of the ordinary cargo. Opium got to be smuggled in. By night. On board a scrambling dragon."

"A scrambling *what*?" I ask him.

"That's what the Chinese call them. The boats the smugglers use got twelve, maybe fourteen oars. They're light, and pretty fast, too. They call them 'scrambling dragons.'"

Then Hawk told me to go see if I could borrow Captain Hiram's spyglass. I was back with it in no time. Hawk and I stood at the starboard bow, looking north, up the bay. The sun was getting ready to set, and some clouds in the west were turning pink.

"See those reddish-colored cliffs? Way up at the head of the bay? That's where the main mouth of the river Pearl empties into the bay. That's the Tiger's Mouth, like they call it."

He handed me the spyglass and I stared at the river and its sandstone cliffs.

"With all that red stone, I guess you could say it looks a *little* bit like a Tiger's Mouth," I tell him.

"And there's forts up there, too. Five of them. You can't see but two of them from here. The other three are further up the river. Supposed to be guarding the entrance. Keeping out foreign devils, like us, and smugglers, and pirates, too. Only trouble is those forts are armed with cannon so old they'd probably blow up if the Chinese was ever to try to *fire* them."

We laughed and joked some about what a big modern British man-o'-war could do to those forts and their antique cannon. Stuck up there, useless, on those cliffs. Scaring nobody.

"Captain Hiram says the Emperor of China is going to be sorry, one of these days. Sorry he didn't spend some money for some good, new guns."

Hawk stretched his huge frame and closed up the spyglass. "But by the time he finds out his mistake, it'll be too late."

He says he overheard Captain Hiram telling Mr. Redmond, the first mate, that it didn't make sense for the Emperor to expect to be able to keep his country all sealed up. With Canton the only city open to trade. Not with the British Navy strong as it is, ready to blast its way in. And everybody else in the world hungry to trade here, too, for China's silks and spices and teas.

"Emperor of China don't know how much trouble he's in," says Hawk, giving me a wink. "Sitting up there in his palace in Peking, pretending he's safe. But not a bit safer, really, than an ostrich burying his head in the sand."

I slip the spyglass back into its case and return it to Uncle Hiram. Then I hurry back to Hawk.

"Looks like we're in for some fog," he says, leaning over the rail and staring back south, down the bay. Sure enough there are ragged gray streaks blowing in from the southeast. Blowing in from the open sea. Lintin Island keeps growing larger the nearer we approach. I can see seven or eight tall sailing ships moored in close to shore.

"They're all waiting there for nightfall," says Hawk. "Just like we'll be doing, in a little while. Waiting till it gets full dark. Listening for the splash of the oars of the scrambling dragons, rowing out to pick up their opium."

I ask Hawk how it is that the Emperor of China can't find a way to put a stop to the opium traffic.

He says the reason is simple enough. Too many merchants in Canton—merchants and government officials—are getting rich on the trade. Getting rich along with all the foreign devil sea captains who are shipping it in. All of them—merchants, smugglers, and sea captains—pay money to the Emperor's officials to turn their heads and look the other way. It is a dangerous arrangement, because the opium trade is strictly against the law. But bribes and huge profits keep it alive and kicking, despite all the dangers.

"So that's the way it works."

"That's the way it works, Sammy," says Hawk.

I must admit I'm surprised. And startled, too. I can't help wondering what Ma would have said if she had known the ins and outs of this opium smuggling business. What a huge part it plays in the high and mighty China trade. And how hard she'd worked to get me into such a devious venture, "through the cabin window."

*   *   *

By now, Lintin Island is only a mile and a half off our port bow. The sun has sunk completely out of sight below the hills on the western shore of the bay. The fog bank has rolled in from the sea and overtaken us. Its thick gray curtain is all we can see when we look astern, south toward Macao.

Captain Hiram calls all hands on deck and orders them to keep a sharp lookout for pirates. It seems they're most likely to try to attack a well-armed foreign ship, like ours, when they can slip up on her under the cover of fog. Captain Hiram says sometimes there's two pirate ships, working together. Sometimes even three!

"They'll use not only ordinary weapons, like pistols and cutlasses," says Captain Hiram, "but stink bombs and firecrackers and gongs and fire!"

By this time Captain Hiram's Chinese pilot has brought the *Orient Venture* into the little bay on Lintin Island where I'd seen the other sailing ships moored. It's not easy to see just how many are lying at anchor, because the fog is growing thicker by the minute.

"All this fog will give the smugglers plenty of cover," I whisper to Hawk.

"Yep. Safer for the scrambling dragons, for sure," says he, "but it gives plenty of cover for pirates, too."

Captain Hiram orders Mr. Redmond to lower away. We hear the splash of the anchor and the rumble of the hawser running out. Then half the crew is ordered aloft to furl the sails on the yards. The other half is sent below, to begin bringing up the chests of opium from the hold.

Hawk and me are in the group working with the chests. It takes all of us nearly an hour to heave them up through the forward hatch, and then to rig up the derrick and winch and pulleys for lowering them over the side.

Time we are all squared away, the first of the scrambling dragons comes scraping alongside the *Orient Venture*.

Captain Hiram and Mr. Redmond won't allow but two men from the scrambling dragon to climb the rope ladder onto the deck of our ship. They have very little to say to one another, and what little they do say, I can't

understand. Captain Hiram studies the papers they give him. From what I can make out, he and Mr. Redmond seem to know these Chinese fellows real well. Probably done business with them before. I think one of them was called Ah Sung.

Hawk and me and all the rest are busy as can be, lowering chests of opium over the side, into the scrambling dragons. The fog is so thick now, we can hardly see to work.

We are right in the midst of lowering the tenth chest over the side when real trouble strikes.

First, something rams the opposite side of the *Orient Venture* so that her timbers creak and shudder. An unearthly screeching breaks out, and we lower that tenth chest of opium into the scrambling dragon so fast I'm sure she'll be swamped.

"Mr. Redmond!" calls Captain Hiram. "Mr. Redmond! We're boarded by pirates! You take the swivel up forward. I'll take this one, aft!"

The two swivel guns begin firing a second or two later. There's shadowy figures swirling through the fog, swarming up over the ship's side. The pirates are throwing grappling hooks, tied to rope ladders, up into the rigging and over the rail. It's hard to make out just

what they're doing, in all that foggy blank-
ness. There's stink bombs exploding, smelling
like spoiled beef and rotten eggs. They're
banging gongs and there's fireworks popping.
Screams and turmoil everywhere on deck.

Three pirates come dropping down from
the rigging overhead. There's more coming up
over the rail. Hawk and I rush over to the
starboard side. He's got a cutlass and a pistol.
All I got is a dagger.

I can see Hawk struggling with four shapes.
His pistol flashes and roars. There's shouting
and screaming and shooting everywhere.

I'm not sure just what happens next. Seems like Hawk is calling out "Sam!" I've lost sight of him and I run along the rail trying to find him. The deck is nothing but fog and wild confusion. Then something comes down hard on my head. And I can feel I'm falling. Falling.

·2·

On Board the
Scrambling Dragon

"Lord have mercy, Sam," says Hawk. "Where do you suppose we are?"

I'm so glad to hear him talk sensible again I could have hugged him.

"You all right, Hawk? You been talking out of your head for an hour or more."

I can feel Hawk heaving at the ropes that bind him.

"I'm not much hurt," he rumbles. "But I'd sure give a heap to know just where I am."

"I reckon the pirates got us," says I.

"Naw, can't be *them*," says he. "Pirates would have killed us, sure. Besides, pirates all got sailing junks. And this thing's being rowed by oars. Can't you hear 'em splashing?"

He's right. I must be a fool not to have been able to figure that out for myself.

"You mean they got us on board the *smugglers'* ship? On one of the scrambling dragons that was alongside . . . ?"

"Probably so," says Hawk. "They must have seen us fall overboard, and fished us out of the bay."

"You reckon we ought to holler?" says I.

"Don't you dare do that!" says Hawk, real fierce. "Don't do that *whatever* you do! You want to get your throat cut? If they got our chests of opium on board this thing, last thing in the world they're going to want is somebody screeching and hollering. How long you reckon we been here?"

I tell him I been awake about an hour, maybe. But I have no idea how long I been lying here senseless before I come to.

"Hungry as I am," says Hawk, "it must have been four or five hours."

"That's right," says I. "We wouldn't have had supper until we *finished* unloading the chests, and . . ."

"Be quiet! Someone's coming!" says Hawk.

It's real dark, here in the hold. But when the man comes up close, I make out that it's the same smuggler Captain Hiram had called Ah Sung. He has a scar that runs from the outer corner of his left eye halfway down to his chin. It pulls the left side of his mouth awry,

in a kind of permanent, horrible grin. He sure isn't smiling. He's angry and scared. So nervous his face is sweating.

Hawk keeps on talking with him for quite a while. He asks him a lot of questions I don't quite understand. They use some kind of halfway English. It sounds like Hawk is saying we want something to eat, something to drink.

"You all same suppose talkee too muchee *soft!*" says Ah Sung. "Suppose talkee too muchee *soft!*"

Then he hurries away.

"He going to bring us something to eat?"

"He says they'll feed us," says Hawk, "once they quit rowing. If we keep real quiet."

"Once they quit rowing?" I say. "When will that be?"

"Probably not for another hour or two. These boats got to make all the time they can by night. Soon as it starts to get light, they have to pull into the riverbank somewhere, and hide. They can't risk traveling by day. Chinese Emperor's got his navy sailing up and down this river. On patrol."

"You mean we're not in the bay no more, Hawk?"

"Didn't I *tell* you, Sammy?" says Hawk, real impatient. "Do I have to explain everything two or three times over? We been in the Pearl River for at least two hours or more. We're halfway up to Whampoa Reach by now, I expect. Least we *should* be."

"Did he say what happened to the ship? In the fight?"

"He don't know," says Hawk. "He couldn't tell me. Soon as the shooting started, Ah Sung cut himself loose from the *Orient Venture* and slipped away in the fog. We're lucky he saw us fall into the water. He took pity on us and fished us out. If it had been the pirates who got us instead, we'd have been dead for certain."

I shiver to hear Hawk remind me. But all I say is, "I sure wish Ah Sung would untie us. My arms ache something awful."

"If your ma knew where you are this minute," says Hawk, "she'd be having fits, boy. Her precious little Sammy, cold and hungry. Tied up in the bottom of a smuggler's skiff, somewhere on the river Pearl, forty miles below Canton . . ."

"What you trying to do, Hawk? Get me worse scared than I already am?"

"Aw, Sammy," says Hawk, real slow and easy. "When you going to quit behaving like a ten-year-old farm boy and start trying to be a man? You should never *thought* about signing

on for a sailor if you didn't want some excitement. Some excitement and some danger.
It's good for the blood."

"Well, you never had *this* happen to you,
did you?" says I. "You never fought no pirates
before. Not in all your times at sea . . ."

Hawk is rolling around, thrashing at his
ropes, trying to get his hands free.

"Be mighty dull if unusual things didn't
keep on happening, for the first time, to all of
us," says he. "All I need right now is some hot
food. And a bath. And a nice big, black cigar."

I keep thinking about what he said for quite

some time. Maybe Hawk can be lonesome, at times, and sing his sad songs, way out at sea. But whatever happens, he sure knows how to make the best of things a whole lot better than I do.

"Guess you got some chance for the hot food," says I. "Maybe even for the big cigar. But you'll have a long wait ahead of you before you get that bath of yours."

Hawk chuckles. I suppose he likes knowing that he's got me to quit feeling sorry for myself. He always *could* make me feel better, with that slow, quiet way of his. That easy way so many big men have.

I lie here telling myself that I'm not going to say another word about how hungry I'm getting. It's so dark we can't see a thing. All we can hear is the splash of oars. Sometimes some gongs and some music. We reckon it must be coming from other boats, passing us by, on the river.

"Wish you could see this river by day," says Hawk. "Just jammed full of all kinds of shipping. Junks, chop boats, egg boats, houseboats, mandarin boats. Floating barbershops, laundry boats, vegetable boats, tea barges, salt barges, floating gambling dens. Even floating duck farms, where they raise ducks for the markets in the city. Looks like half of

China bought themselves a boat, and come down here to live on this river."

"I sure wish I could see some of that," says I. "When you reckon they'll untie us and let us go?"

"Ah Sung wouldn't tell me that," says Hawk. "But he might turn us loose at Whampoa Reach. He might, I mean, if we lucky." Hawk gives another huge wrench at the ropes on his arms. His muscles knot up tremendous, but the ropes hold.

Captain Hiram had told me all about Whampoa Reach. Now I'm lying here, wondering what's happened to him. Him and all the men on the *Orient Venture*. I keep wishing I knew how that fight with the pirates finished, back there at Lintin Island. My mind keeps going back to it, again and again.

Uncle Hiram had told me that Whampoa Reach was located on that big bend where the river Pearl turns westward, toward Canton. There's an island in the river there, with a town on it called Whampoa. It's twelve miles below Canton. They say the name Whampoa means "Yellow Anchorage" in Chinese.

Whampoa's the place where all the ships belonging to us foreign devils have to heave to and drop anchor. The Emperor won't let us sail right up to Canton. Afraid one of those British or Yankee ships might decide to bombard the city, I suppose.

Anyway, everybody has to anchor at Whampoa Reach. And all the cargo has to be rowed the rest of the way upriver to Canton, in chop boats. Ferried up, by the Chinese. And there's a whole lot of forms to be filled out, and papers to be signed, and bribes and fees to be paid, and gifts to be given. They call the gifts *cumshaw*. And a lot of stuff that Dave Woolsey, our supercargo, would know all about. If Dave and them weren't killed at Lintin Island, I mean.

Hawk is still thumping around beside me, tearing and straining against his ropes. I can hear him panting. I'm scared he's going to hurt himself.

"Hey, Hawk," I say, "what's it like in Canton?"

"Never seen it, to tell the God's truth," says Hawk, panting real hard. "Never been inside the walls. Never seen nothing but the hongs."

"The hongs?" I say. "What's that?"

And Hawk stops lashing and wrenching at his ropes, just like I hoped he would. He explains to me that each foreign country has a space set aside right there on the riverbank, with a building to itself. A stone-walled

warehouse on the ground floor, and sleeping rooms above, built of wood. On the roof of each of the hongs, they fly their country's flag. So these are the hongs: the American hong, the British hong, the Dutch hong, and like that. Foreign devils like us aren't supposed to go anywhere else in the city, but stay right there on the riverbank, where the hongs are.

"They got some shops, too, where sailors can buy gimcracks and presents and clothes and silk and stuff," says Hawk. "And some grog shops where you can get drunk in a hurry. They sell a lot of hot food, too, in the alleyways. And the streets are hung with shop signs. Crowded with people coming and going. And there's thirteen Chinese merchants—they call them the co-hong merchants. They got their warehouses there, on the riverbank, too. All of them stuffed to over-flowing with tea and silk and chinaware. That's all I ever seen of Canton. Just the edge of it, down by the hongs."

For quite a while I keep thinking about what Hawk has just told me. Wondering what I'm going to say when I get back to New-buryport, Massachusetts. If I ever *do* get back. And Ma or somebody should ask me what I seen in Canton. And I'll have to answer that all I got to look at was a bunch of grog shops and warehouses. Strung out along some muddy riverbank. And I never got inside Canton at all!

* * *

About half an hour later we hear footsteps coming down into the hold where we're lying. Seems to me that the darkness isn't quite so black as it was before. I can make out Ah Sung's scarred face a bit more clearly this time. And I'm pretty sure that the other man with him is probably the other fellow I'd seen at Lintin Island, talking with Captain Hiram on the deck of the *Orient Venture*.

The two men talk a bit, in whispers, with Hawk. Then they begin to untie us!

"Hey, Hawk, what'd they say?" I holler.

"Sam, you be quiet," he answers, in a low, savage growl.

When my wrists are untied, the blood comes rushing back into my hands and they begin to ache something awful.

"Ah Sung says we can come up out of the hold and lie down and get some air," says Hawk. "If we keep out of sight, under the matting, and don't do no loud talking."

I stumble up out of the darkness and lie down beside Hawk, half hidden behind a bale of sugar cane. The opium chests must be hidden down in the darkness, where we've just come from, I reckon. There are stars overhead, and I can see the sweep of the huge muddy river.

Twelve oarsmen, six on a side, are sweating away at the oars. The sky is beginning to grow pale in the east. There's a hilly island coming up, ahead of us. On one of the slopes I can see a pagoda. And there's a good-sized town down at the river's edge. Thirty or forty of our kind of Western sailing ships are moored in the bend of the river. Hawk and I keep straining to see if we can make out the lines of the *Orient Venture.* She doesn't seem to be there, but we're still too far away to be absolutely certain.

The water is beginning to show the first faint pink light of dawn.

"Whampoa Reach," says Hawk in a low rumble beside me.

"We'll soon be putting in to shore," says I, "now that it's getting light."

"Yep," says Hawk. "We'll have to. Either that or risk getting caught by the Emperor's patrols. Ah Sung wouldn't want *that* to happen, Sammy. 'Cause he likes his head right where it is, sitting up there on his shoulders."

Then Hawk tells me that if our scrambling dragon were caught, with all this opium on board, Ah Sung and all his smugglers would be dead men. Marched off to the square in front of the British hong, in Canton, and made to kneel down in the dust, with their hands tied behind them. And each of their heads sliced off at a single blow. By the stroke of the sword of the governor's headsman. Right there in public, in front of the hongs, for all the foreign devils to see. And tremble.

By now we've come up much closer to the ships in the bend of the river. There's thirty-seven vessels on the pink water, swinging at their moorings at Whampoa Reach.

"You see her, Hawk?" I whisper. But it's a fool question. I know she isn't there, before he answers.

"Naw, she ain't here, boy," says Hawk, rough and stern as usual. But the sound of his voice is a lot kinder when he adds, "She must be down below us. She be up tomorrow."

And I can tell he's just as worried as I am. Maybe we'll never see her again. It just might be that—in spite of her swivel guns and her cannon—the pirates captured the *Orient Venture*. Captured the ship and all her crew. Maybe killed them all!

* * *

Off to the right, opposite Whampoa Island, we can see rice paddies and hills and groves of bamboo. There are willows growing at the river's edge. I see a man fishing from his houseboat, using a black cormorant with a

ring around his neck. The ring keeps the huge
bird from swallowing the fish he catches. And
the man pulls the wriggling fish from the
bird's gullet, and drops it into a wicker
basket.

Suddenly we see Ah Sung run back to the
steersman in the stern. He's calling out, real
loud, pointing upriver. The scrambling dragon makes straight for the bank. Ah Sung has
his oarsmen racing for shore. And next thing
we know, we're snugly hidden from view, behind a thick grove of willows.

"What's all this about, Hawk?" says I.
"Why do they look so scared?"

"Hummph," says Hawk, scratching his
side. "Now maybe we get some food. Look
yonder. Up there, boy. That's a mandarin

boat coming downriver. Part of the Emperor of China's navy. On patrol."

There, rounding the bend above Whampoa Island, I see a tall, two-masted junk, with rattan sails. She's red and black, with three banks of oars. She has long red streamers flying from her yards, lettered with Chinese characters worked in gold. Her oarsmen are chanting in rhythm, and gongs are sounding, keeping time for the beat of the oars. From the top of the taller of her two masts she's flying a triangular flag. It's got a yellow dragon on a black field. And the dragon is clutching at a red disc with one of its outstretched claws.

"That's what Ah Sung wanted to avoid," says Hawk, nodding toward the ship. I can see why. Her decks are glittering with soldiers in armor, carrying the cruelest kinds of sharp steel hooks and axes and swords.

She passes by, nearly a mile away. She never even suspects we're hiding here behind the willow grove. I'm mighty thankful for that. Hawk figures we'll probably be hiding here all the rest of today. Until an hour or two after sunset.

I guess he's right. Because now Ah Sung's men are lighting charcoal stoves and beginning to boil water for rice and tea. And I can smell some kind of fish frying.

·3·

In Canton, at the American Hong

The higher the sun climbs in the sky, the more crowded the river becomes with traffic. Boats of all kinds are plying upriver toward Canton, and down toward the Tiger's Mouth at the head of the bay.

After we finish our breakfast of rice and fried fish, Hawk and I go back to our makeshift observation post, near the gunwale of the scrambling dragon. There on the deck, half hidden behind some bales of sugar cane, we keep staring across at the long, curving line of ships anchored at Whampoa Reach. Hoping to catch a glimpse of the *Orient Venture* at anchor, or making her way around the distant bend of the river Pearl. But there's no sign of her.

"You suppose the pirates took her, Hawk?"

"I doubt it," says he. "I doubt it very se-
riously."

But he's frowning and I can see he's more
worried than he wants me to know. Our
scrambling dragon is still tied to the bank,
hidden deep in the willow grove.

"You think we could swim the current
here?" I ask him. "Across to Whampoa Island?"

"Not a chance, Sam," he growls. "Besides,
Ah Sung may pretend to be foolish and
friendly and all. But he doesn't trust us. Not
in the least bit. He's got somebody watching
us every blessed minute, in case you aren't
aware of it."

It was true. Just a few yards away sat one of
the smugglers—to all appearances innocently
mending a rope. But quietly keeping guard on
us, though he seemed to be paying us no
notice whatever.

"What do you reckon they'll do with us,
Hawk?" I whisper.

"We'll just have to wait and see," says he,
"unless we can take the matter out of their
hands, and make us a plan for our own
selves."

I have to admire the quiet, even way he says
it. Just as calm as if he was asking for another
slice of pie. I sit there wondering just what it

would take to put a real scare into Hawk Hollings, but I can't imagine what that might be.

We keep straining our eyes downriver in hopes of seeing the *Orient Venture* beating her way up against the current. But she doesn't show. I begin to get sleepy around the middle of the afternoon. Hawk has been telling me about the thirteen co-hong merchants who control all the trade, up in Canton.

"How come the Emperor keeps everything so tight in his fist, Hawk?"

"I don't know," says he. "He probably makes those thirteen merchants pay him plenty of money for the privilege of trading with us foreign devils. And I been told he wants to keep as much distance as possible between his people and us. He don't want us coming here changing the way the Chinese been doing things for thousands and thousands of years."

Hawk goes on talking about how us foreign devils aren't allowed to mix with the Chinese in the city. How we aren't even allowed, by law, to try to learn Chinese. And how the Chinese are forbidden to learn our languages, too.

"That's why we all got to speak this foolishness called 'pidgin English,'" says Hawk. "That kind of talk you heard me and Ah Sung talking."

"Why do they call it 'pidgin'?" I ask him.

"Because that's close as they come to say-ing 'business English.' When they say 'busi-ness' it comes out 'pidgin.'"

Then Hawk tells me that the leader of those thirteen hong merchants is a rich old fellow named Houqua.

"They say he's one of the richest men in the world," says Hawk, "but I wouldn't know about that. Your uncle, Captain Dwight, he's been to dinner at old Houqua's house. Had every kind of good something to eat served to him, he told us. In a great big house all sur-rounded with lakes and fishponds and trees and every kind of flower. Yes, they say old Houqua's worth millions and millions of dollars."

I just let Hawk talk on and on, while the afternoon sun drops lower in the western sky. There's no point trying to interrupt him. We got nothing to do, anyway, until evening comes, and the smugglers start upriver again. With our illegal cargo of opium.

Opium that the Chinese call "foreign mud," according to Hawk. And *dangerous* mud, too, I'd say.

Captain Hiram had told me a lot about Houqua, on those long days while we was slowly crossing the Pacific. He said that any promise made by the old hong merchant was just as good as gold. So good was his word that no Yankee captain ever bothered to inspect any merchandise coming from

Houqua's hong. If a chest or a bale were stamped with Houqua's chop mark, so:

浩 官

the customer could be sure he was getting chests of the very finest quality hyson tea. Or the very same bales of embroidered silk that he had inspected in Houqua's warehouse, and paid for in advance. Without having to bother to break them open and make certain. For Houqua had never been known to cheat anyone he dealt with.

"Just wait till you see Canton, boy," says Hawk. "It's ten times busier and bigger than New York or Philadelphia. Twenty times bigger, for all I know."

I lie here, staring at the ships at Whampoa Reach, just wishing I *could* see Canton right this minute. Either that, or the *Orient Venture.* Anything to lift my spirits and make me believe that we'll find a way to get off this dirty little vessel. And say goodbye to Ah Sung forever.

* * *

Soon as me and Hawk are finished eating our supper, Ah Sung does something real sneaky. Half of the crew comes up behind us, real quiet, in the shadows. Six of them jump Hawk, from behind, and truss him up in no time. Two of them take care of me.

Then they split open two bales of sugar cane and pack me and Hawk inside of them. Loose, I mean. Just so we're hidden. Then they tie gags on our mouths and close up the bales.

I lie here, struggling, for an hour or so. I keep hearing the steady splash of the oars. Ah Sung is in a terrible hurry to get his boat up-river.

Better not to think of the curses I'm wasting on Ah Sung and the rest of his crew. Hawk

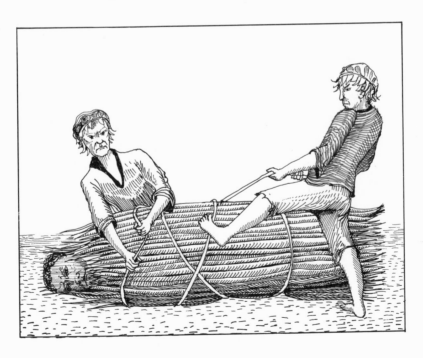

and I should have guessed. We should have *known* they wouldn't have risked leaving us loose, on deck, when they rowed upriver into the night, on the final leg of their journey.

My hands are aching like thunder again. And my throat is dry, because of the gag. And after what seems like an hour, I begin drifting off to sleep . . .

* * *

It's still dark when I awake. Not that I could see anything anyway, bundled up like I am in this bale of cane. But there's something must have woke me up. A jolt or something.

"You all right, Sammy?" Hawk growls. Real deep. Real low. He's got rid of his gag! I try to make a sound, even with my gag still in my mouth.

"Don't make any noise," he whispers. And I feel him opening the bale. I roll out onto the deck, and he gets rid of my gag. And then my hands are loose.

"Hawk, how did you . . .?"

He clamps his huge hand over my mouth and I nod my head I understand.

"We're not far from Canton," Hawk whispers. "Another hour. Maybe less. They making good time. I don't know where they're going or what they planning to do with us. But

we're not going to wait to find out. Time this
boat gets up opposite the hongs . . ."

And Hawk begins whispering his plans, real
low. Just like a Napoleon or some other kind
of big general.

"First we come to this little round stone
fort, on an island in the middle of the river.
Nobody uses it no more. The Dutch built it
years ago. They call it Dutch Folly Fort. Five
minutes past that, we'll see the lights of the
hongs, on the right bank . . ."

We sit there, beside the sugar cane bales,
hiding in the shadows. Listening to the splash
of the oars. Ah Sung's scrambling dragon is
hurrying upriver fast as it can go.

There's no moon tonight. But there's plenty
of river traffic. Lights from the lanterns on the
different boats shimmer over the dark water.
Our scrambling dragon is completely dark.
But we can see a little, by the lights of the
others passing by.

Then I see the dim round shape of Dutch
Folly Fort, looming up in the middle of the
river.

"We're nearly to the hongs," Hawk whispers. "Now listen carefully, Sammy . . ."

He's broken open one of the chests of
opium. And he's got maybe seven or eight of
those big melon-shaped balls sitting beside

us. Opium! Foreign mud! The cause of all our
trouble . . .

"Sammy, the hongs will come up on the
right," says Hawk. "And soon as they do, we
heave these balls of opium over the *left* side.
You understand? To distract their attention
to port?"

I'm not sure I do, but I say yes, anyhow. I
suppose I should have known Hawk would
think of *something*. He always does.

The fort slips past on the left and in a mo-
ment it's gone. The tempo of the beat of the
oars grows quicker and our scrambling
dragon picks up speed.

Now I can see them, off to the right! The hongs of the foreign devils! A row of buildings not too far back from the river. Most of them showing lights in their upper stories.

"Right now!" says Hawk. And he heaves his first opium ball off to the left. It splashes into the river. Now I'm throwing mine. And Hawk heaves the rest of his into the river Pearl.

Ah Sung comes up from below and hurries over to the port gunwale, calling softly to another member of his crew.

But by that time Hawk and me are dropping over the starboard side, into the muddy waters of the river Pearl. And we start swimming for dear life. For the hongs, a quarter of a mile away.

* * *

I guess I would have drowned if it hadn't been for Hawk helping me two or three times, when the current got real strong.

The river was real dirty and it stank.

I suppose Ah Sung missed us, soon enough. But he had to get further upriver with his opium. He certainly couldn't risk landing it at the hongs. And he didn't want any noise or disturbance, dangerous as his business was. So he just let us slip away, and he never turned back to try to recapture us.

Hawk had figured it all out in his head! Trust him!

We crawled up onto the nasty, muddy bank in front of the hongs, like two drowned rats. Well, I was a drowned rat. I remember lying there, gasping for breath. With Hawk still fresh as a daisy.

He knows exactly where to go. We cross the empty square—he says its *full* of porters and workmen and soldiers and food-sellers and foreign devils by day—and we walk up Hog Lane.

Hog Lane is the narrow little street where sailors come when they're on leave from their ships. To buy souvenirs and clothes and gim-cracks and ivory fans and paper flowers and caged birds. And all kinds of silk and stuff. They can get drunk here, too, which plenty of them do.

Right now its dark and late and most of the shops are closed for the night. Hawk wants to get to the American hong, on Old China Street, so he hurries me along.

We slip through the dark alleys, all their shops closed up and shuttered.

"So many people here during the day you can hardly pass," says Hawk, clamping his big arm around me, so's I can't fall behind. It

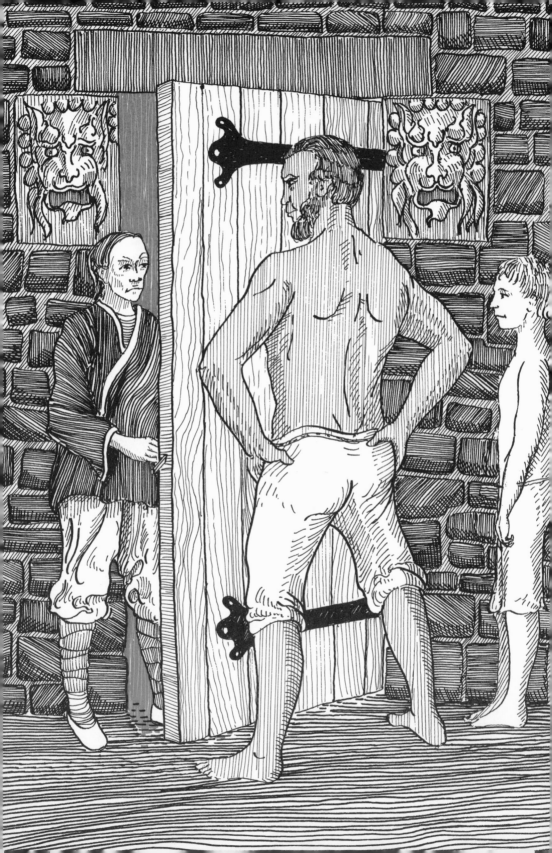

sure is hard trying to keep up with his big strides, and I practically have to run.

At last we stop in front of a heavy wooden door, set into a blank stone wall. I hear a funny wooden rattling noise nearby.

"What's that, Hawk?"

"That's the night watchman in the street, shaking his wooden clapper. Supposed to scare away thieves. They got plenty of *them* in this place."

Then he throws himself on the wooden door, hollering and pounding.

A Chinese servant opens the door only after Hawk curses him for a full ten minutes, seems like, to me.

Once we're inside they take us upstairs, and we meet a plain little Yankee gentleman, kind of tall and scrawny, named Mr. Ward Collins. He's got a fringe of white hair around a shiny bald spot. Mr. Collins has his servants bring us some rice and some stewed-up meat and vegetables. We go out onto a verandah overlooking the river Pearl and eat our supper there. It sure is better than Ah Sung's fried fish.

"You're lucky to be alive," says Mr. Collins, with a shrewd glance at Hawk and me. "They might just as soon have killed you, you know. It's dangerous, smuggling opium."

"That's what I figured," says Hawk. "That's why me and Sammy said goodbye the way we did, and swam ashore."

I hadn't realized we was in that much danger. But I'm sure glad that *Hawk* knew! We could have been dead by now . . .

Mr. Ward Collins talks kind of dry and slow. And he's real businesslike and sensible. I tell him that I'm Captain Hiram Dwight's nephew. And he's got some good news for us, about the *Orient Venture.*

"Your uncle's ship is safe," says he. "We got word about her late this afternoon. She's moored downriver, at Whampoa Reach. They drove off the pirates at Lintin Island. There was some damage from fire, but they saved the ship, the crew, and the entire cargo. Nobody hurt except Mr. Redmond, the first mate. His arm was broken by a bullet."

* * *

Next morning, around ten o'clock, Uncle Hiram himself is hugging me, in the American hong, in Canton.

"You know, Ward," says he to Mr. Collins, "I thought we'd lost this boy for sure. And Hollings, too."

"Take more than a couple of pirates and smugglers," says Hawk, in his deep rumble.

There's a lot of talk about the battle with the pirates in the fog, off Lintin Island. And a lot of questions about what happened to Hawk and me once we was on board Ah Sung's scrambling dragon.

"You know who'll be selling that opium, eventually?" says Captain Hiram to Mr. Collins.

"Tell me," says he.

"None other than that old rascal, the head of the co-hong merchants, Houqua."

Hawk and I look at one another but we don't smile. We've had too much trouble with the opium traffic to see anything funny in it. And I start to wondering what Houqua will do if the Emperor ever finds out that he's mixed up in smuggling foreign mud into his imperial Flowery Kingdom.

* * *

We got a couple of weeks for seeing the sights, Hawk and me, before Captain Hiram and Dave Woolsey, his supercargo, can buy everything they need for the homeward voyage. So we spend the time together, poking around the hongs.

One morning we go over to Houqua's hong, on Lob-lob Creek, to watch his servants packing tea. First they weigh it out, and then they stow it into lead-lined, brassbound wooden chests. And a couple of men trample it in real tight, with their bare feet!

There's lots of chinaware, too—dishes and tea sets and punch bowls—being carefully crated up, wrapped in straw and rice paper.

And there's bales and bales and bales of silk. Some of it gauzy. Some of it ribbed and heavy. Some of it painted with flowers and birds. Some of it stitched with embroidery.

"When the ladies see that stuff," says Hawk, with a chuckle, "it will fetch a pile of money, back home."

I reckon it will. But I keep thinking about the opium we brought into this strange heathen land. And all the damage it will cause.

I keep wondering what Ma would say if she understood the whole system. The way it works here in Canton. That, and how nobody seems to care—so long as it all makes money.

Captain Hiram and Dave Woolsey seem to be real pleased with the way the trade has been going. All the furs and silver dollars and ginseng root and sandalwood that we had stored in the hold of the *Orient Venture* has been rowed upriver, by now, in chop boats from Whampoa Reach. It's all stowed away, safe, in the stone warehouse, downstairs. Here in the American hong, on Old China

Street. Dave says he's getting a good price for the whole lot.

Mr. Ward Collins says that the tea crop is especially good this season. So Dave is buying a great deal of it—both the black and the green. He has also purchased a bit more than nine tons of silk—which is the legal limit that the Chinese will allow any one foreign ship to carry away.

"You know what they pack down at the very bottom of the hold, Sammy?" says Hawk. "You know what goes down first, where the bilge water can't ruin it?"

I don't know, so Hawk has to tell me. It's the crates of china! The dishes and the tea sets! On top of that they pack the silk and the tea. Mr. Ward Collins tells us that the china-ware is so cheap it don't matter much if some of it gets broken. It's much more important to keep the silk and the tea dry. "Because that's *really* worth something," says he.

* * *

One day Hawk and me get a glimpse of Houqua, when Captain Hiram goes over to his hong to give him a special present: a barrel of Madeira wine and ten specially nice sea otter skins.

He's a thin little fellow, with a wispy white

beard. He wears a silk robe and a long string of pearls nearly about as big as grapes. He's real polite, too. Hawk would have made about six of him, I reckon. But there's no doubt about it, Houqua's a millionaire, three or four times over.

Mr. Collins says we should have been here last year, if we wanted to be in on some real excitement. That was when the great fire struck, and burned down all the hongs. All but Houqua's, that is. I guess you got to be lucky, as well as smart, to be rich. Hawk says it ain't worth worrying about. I reckon he knows best. Anyway, I don't plan to try to get rich, myself, if you got to smuggle opium to get there. And Hawk and me, we've had enough excitement *this* year, even though we missed the fire.

* * *

Mr. Ward Collins helps us pass some of the time—while we're waiting for them to load the *Orient Venture*—teaching me and Hawk a little bit about Chinese writing.

Sitting out on the verandah of the American hong, watching all the river traffic at Canton swarming up and down, Hawk and me are practicing our brush strokes.

Here's the way they write man: 人

and woman: 女

This is east: 東 and this is west: 西

This is tea: 茶

This is silk: 絲

This is porcelain: 磁 器

And here's the one for opium: 鴉 片

Soon as Captain Hiram has the *Orient Venture* full to the brim with tea and silk, he's ready to get his papers in order and sail for home.

The Chinese officials give him his clearance—a mark they call "the grand chop." It looks like this: 戧 記

As soon as his papers are stamped with that mark, all of us are rowed downriver to Whampoa Reach. It sure is good to see the *Orient Venture*, swinging at her mooring.

* * *

Next day, Captain Hiram drops down the river, passes through the Tiger's Mouth, and sails out into the bay. There's no fog this time when we pass by Lintin Island. And no pirates. But there's plenty of ships there unloading chests of opium.

Captain Hiram says we're going to thread our way south through the islands, into the Indian Ocean. And go home around Africa's Cape of Good Hope. It will take us about eight weeks. Maybe more.

Hawk and me spend a lot of time together. He's the same old Hawk as ever. Playing his accordion. Singing his sad, lonely songs. Scrubbing himself all over, with that soapy

sponge in a hot bath, three times a day. I never *see* such a man for washing.

And after he's nearly scrubbed the skin right off himself, every evening of the world he sends me up to the galley. Asking the cook for another tub of hot water.

The *Orient Venture* has rounded Africa, and is in the South Atlantic now. Heading north, for Massachusetts. Loaded with silk and tea.

Me and Hawk are up on deck, under the stars. Laughing and joking. Washing our clothes.

About this Story

Although this story is fiction, it is largely based on fact. It should be imagined as happening in the early 1820s. For—roughly from the close of the American Revolution up until the Civil War—hundreds and hundreds of American sea captains sailed to Canton, in the China trade.

They carried with them silver, furs, ginseng, sandalwood—and opium. And they brought home with them valuable cargoes of porcelain, silk, spices, and tea. Many of the earliest fortunes in America were amassed in this exotic trade with Canton.

Old imperial China was distinctly hostile to the British, Americans, Dutch, and other Europeans who came to her shores. Foreigners' warehouses, or hongs, were confined to a narrow strip of land on the north bank of the Pearl River, just outside the walls of Canton. Movement was restricted; they were not permitted to travel anywhere in the interior, and no city but Canton was open to them, for trade.

All purchases had to pass through the hands of the thirteen co-hong merchants, in Canton, which was headed by the merchant prince Houqua (1769–1843), who was probably the richest merchant in the world, in his day.

There really were pirates (called "foam of the sea" by the Chinese) infesting the coasts of the Flowery Kingdom. And they often attacked ships of the foreign devils—the *fan kwae*—as well as those of the Chinese merchants.

Smugglers did indeed carry chests of opium up-river in swiftly rowed vessels, called "scrambling dragons," from Lintin Island, up the Pearl River, and so on into the interior.

So much opium poured into China, in fact, that the Emperor tried to put a stop to the trade, and in 1838 ordered all stores of "foreign mud" confiscated. His action resulted in the Opium War (1839–42), in which Britain sent a fleet of warships to China. Their cannon smashed the useless forts with their ancient guns, supposedly guarding the Tiger's Mouth, and ascended the Pearl River to Canton. There they bombarded and burned the city. The British remained until China promised to open five ports to the trade, and to pay the *British* an indemnity which ran into the millions.

The Emperor forced Houqua, alone, to pay two million dollars toward the cost of this indemnity, and a year later the harassed and brokenhearted old merchant prince was dead.

Special Note Regarding Pidgin English: "Pidgin English" was a kind of basic trade dialect used at the hongs—*not* because the Chinese were in any way incapable of learning to speak foreign languages to perfection; but rather because the Emperor and his mandarins forbade them to study European languages systematically, because they wanted to keep as much distance as possible between the Chinese co-hong merchants and the foreign devils. Despite their efforts, many friendships in the nineteenth century developed between the Chinese and the *fan kwae*.

F.N.M.